LEGACY

Women Poets
OF THE
Harlem Renaissance

Also by Nikki Grimes

Planet Middle School
One Last Word
Southwest Sunrise

LEGACY

Women Poets
OF THE
Harlem Renaissance

—— ■ ——

NIKKI GRIMES

ARTWORK BY
Vanessa Brantley-Newton · Cozbi A. Cabrera · Nina Crews
Pat Cummings · Laura Freeman · Jan Spivey Gilchrist · Ebony Glenn
Xia Gordon · April Harrison · Vashti Harrison · Ekua Holmes
Cathy Ann Johnson · Keisha Morris · Daria Peoples-Riley · Andrea Pippins
Erin Robinson · Shadra Strickland · Nicole Tadgell · Elizabeth Zunon

BLOOMSBURY
CHILDREN'S BOOKS
NEW YORK LONDON OXFORD NEW DELHI SYDNEY

BLOOMSBURY CHILDREN'S BOOKS
Bloomsbury Publishing Inc., part of Bloomsbury Publishing Plc
1385 Broadway, New York, NY 10018

BLOOMSBURY, BLOOMSBURY CHILDREN'S BOOKS, and the Diana logo are trademarks of
Bloomsbury Publishing Plc

First published in the United States of America in January 2021
by Bloomsbury Children's Books

Text copyright © 2021 by Nikki Grimes
All illustrations © 2021 by the following: Ekua Holmes (page 17), Shadra Strickland (page 21),
Andrea Pippins (page 25), Xia Gordon (page 29), Nina Crews (page 33), Cathy Ann Johnson (page 37),
Vashti Harrison (page 43), Daria Peoples-Riley (page 47), Elizabeth Zunon (page 51),
Cozbi A. Cabrera (page 55), Erin Robinson (page 59), Nicole Tadgell (page 63),
Vanessa Brantley-Newton (page 69), April Harrison (page 73), Jan Spivey Gilchrist (page 77),
Ebony Glenn (page 81), Pat Cummings (page 85), Laura Freeman (page 89), Keisha Morris (page 93)

Citiscape illustration on pages 10–11, 38–39, 64–65, and 96–97: irsy/Shutterstock.com

Bloomsbury books may be purchased for business or promotional use. For information on bulk purchases
please contact Macmillan Corporate and Premium Sales Department at specialmarkets@macmillan.com

Names: Grimes, Nikki, author. | Cabrera, Cozbi A., illustrator.
Title: Legacy : women poets of the Harlem Renaissance / by Nikki Grimes ;
artwork by Cozbi A. Cabrera [and 18 others].
Description: New York : Bloomsbury, 2021. | Includes bibliographical references and index.
Summary: From Children's Literature Legacy Award–winning author Nikki Grimes comes a feminist-
forward new collection of poetry celebrating the little-known women poets of the Harlem Renaissance—
paired with full-color, original art from today's most talented female African American illustrators.
Identifiers: LCCN 2020024833 (print) | LCCN 2020024834 (e-book)
ISBN 978-1-68119-944-3 (hardcover) • ISBN 978-1-68119-945-0 (e-book)
Subjects: LCSH: American poetry—African American women authors. |
African Americans—Juvenile poetry. | Harlem Renaissance—Influence.
Classification: LCC PS3557.R489982 L44 2021 (print) | LCC PS3557.R489982 (e-book) |
DDC 811/.54—dc23
LC record available at https://lccn.loc.gov/2020024833
LC e-book record available at https://lccn.loc.gov/2020024834

Book design by John Candell
Printed in China by Leo Paper Products, Heshan, Guangdong
2 4 6 8 10 9 7 5 3 1

All papers used by Bloomsbury Publishing Plc are natural, recyclable products made from wood
grown in well-managed forests. The manufacturing processes conform to the environmental
regulations of the country of origin.

To find out more about our authors and books visit www.bloomsbury.com and sign up for our newsletters.

For Tonya Bolden, Carole Boston Weatherford,
and Cheryl Hudson for their commitment to rescue,
and celebrate, female Black voices from the past.

TABLE OF CONTENTS

LEGACY

Women Poets
OF THE
Harlem Renaissance

PREFACE

For centuries, accomplished women, of all races, have fallen out of the historical records. In the music realm, for example, we've long known and lauded the name and compositions of Wolfgang Amadeus Mozart, but few are familiar with his equally gifted sister, Maria Anna Mozart, a superb instrumentalist and composer in her own right.

In the sciences, we were taught the names of astronauts like John Glenn, but few could recite the names of early NASA scientists, mathematicians, and engineers like Katherine Johnson, Dorothy Vaughan, Mary Jackson, and Christine Darden, who helped to make Glenn's successful orbit of the earth possible. It took the Oscar-nominated Hollywood movie *Hidden Figures*, based on a book by Margot Lee Shetterly, to bring these groundbreaking women to light.

Going farther back in time, Hatshepsut, the only female pharaoh, all but disappeared from history until recent years. It should come as no surprise, then, that the names of gifted, even prolific, women poets of the Harlem Renaissance are little known, especially as compared to their male counterparts. Ask a well-read person to name male poets of the period, and they're likely to rattle off Countee Cullen, Paul Laurence Dunbar, and Langston Hughes without skipping a beat. Ask the same readers to list women poets of the period, and you'll likely hear the sound of crickets. Georgia Douglas Johnson, Jessie Redmon Fauset, and Gwendolyn Bennett might possibly come to mind, after careful thought, but what about Mae V. Cowdery, author of *We Lift Our Voices and Other Poems*, or Anne Spencer, Effie Lee Newsome, Esther Popel, or Alice Dunbar-Nelson, once the wife of Paul Laurence Dunbar? These women not only produced poetry during this period, but several of them were editors of the literary magazines and anthologies in which Cullen, Hughes, Dunbar—and their female counterparts—were featured.

In these pages, you will meet some of the gifted female poets—and remarkable women—of the Harlem Renaissance who created alongside and often nurtured the male poets we know. They didn't all produce poetry collections of their own, but each played an integral part in this historic era in America.

I hope you enjoy the work of these poets, and the Golden Shovel poems they inspired me to write.

THE HARLEM RENAISSANCE

The Harlem Renaissance was one of the most remarkable periods of artistic growth and exploration in American history. This era followed the first wave of the Great Migration, when 750,000 African Americans left the South in search of a better life. Many of them settled in Harlem, where they finally felt free to express themselves and speak their minds without fear, and one of the ways they did so was through the arts. These were the sterling days of such luminaries as James Weldon Johnson, performer Josephine Baker, and artist Aaron Douglas. Wow!

The beginning of the Harlem Renaissance also coincided with the Nineteenth Amendment, giving women the right to vote. While Jim Crow laws and overt voter suppression lessened the impact of Black women going to the polls, the heady atmosphere created by this new world order was surely felt by them as well. Keep in mind, Black suffragettes fought for a woman's right to vote, too.

During this period, an increasing number of women—Black and white—began pursuing their education. This was a major shift. Whereas before, large percentages of African American working women were limited to domestic trades (their skin color kept most from being hired in factories), more were graduating from school to enter professions as nurses and teachers. From this same pool, female novelists, essayists, playwrights, and poets were emerging—a new literati. African American women were finding their voices. They wrote boldly about race, earnestly questioned the white standards of beauty that cast them as ugly, and forged a new sense of place as they began to explore all that they could be, and what a challenge that was for those pursuing careers in the arts.

In the article "Double Bind: Three Women of the Harlem Renaissance," author Anthony Walton wrote, "The women poets of the Harlem Renaissance faced one of the classic American double-binds: they were Black, and they were female, during an epoch when the building of an artistic career for anyone of either of those identities was a considerable challenge." These words captured precisely what the women writers of the Harlem Renaissance were up against. And still, they rose.

Between 1918 and 1937, an explosion of African American art and literature spread from one big city to another. In Harlem that number included Zora Neale Hurston and Angelina Weld Grimké. In nearby Washington, DC, Georgia Douglas Johnson and Jessie Redmon Fauset held court. However, a number of extraordinary women poets of the period, poets like Blanche Taylor Dickinson, Mae V. Cowdery, and Esther Popel, are usually left off that roster. As it happens, many more African American women poets than we're familiar with found a home for their artistic self-expression in Black-owned magazines and literary journals like *Fire!!*, cofounded by Gwendolyn Bennett; *Opportunity: A Journal of Negro Life*, edited by Charles S. Johnson; and *The Crisis*, edited by W. E. B. Du Bois for twenty-four years. For this last journal, novelist and poet Jessie Redmon Fauset served as literary editor. In fact, Black-owned newspapers and journals sprang up throughout the northern states. It was there, removed from the daily constrictions of Jim Crow laws and the constant threat of violence from the Ku Klux Klan, that African Americans spread their cultural wings and began to fly.

Personal essays, fiction, plays, and poetry reflecting racial pride began to take center stage, while the first glimpses of Black life, as seen from a Black perspective, came to the fore. Women writers, especially, also brought in poetry about nature, their connection to the earth, and the rediscovery of their power as women. Together with the music, dance, and visual art created by African Americans during this era, the groundbreaking literature that rose from the Harlem Renaissance proved to America, and the world, that there was more to the minds, hearts, and souls of Black folk than previously expressed.

Through the decades, this literature has reminded readers, Black and white, how vital it is that we define ourselves, set our own paths, celebrate our own strengths, and determine our own destiny, no matter what obstacles are placed in our way.

I have been honored to attend the Coretta Scott King Book Awards Breakfast on many occasions, and whenever I rise to join in the refrain of "Lift Every Voice and Sing" by James Weldon Johnson, I feel the pull of the tether that connects me to the Harlem Renaissance. The art and literature of that era still resonates today.

This seems like a good time to bring more of the women's voices from the Harlem Renaissance to the fore. And there are more of them than you might imagine. Even I was surprised at their numbers. I chose as many as I could for inclusion here.

These literary lights wrote at a time of racial profiling, though the term had not yet been coined. They witnessed and read about racial violence and every variety of injustice imaginable. This was a time when lynchings of Black men filled the news, and the women who loved those men had cause to fear. Yet these women gathered their inner strength and ascended to great heights, in spite of all. They helped to lay the foundation for Gwendolyn Brooks, Maya Angelou, Toni Morrison, and the many other Black women writers who followed. I draw from that strength.

POETRY FORM

The form I used to create this book is called the Golden Shovel, a form originated by poet Terrance Hayes. I've used this style previously in the poetry collection *One Last Word*: *Wisdom from the Harlem Renaissance* and the picture book *The Watcher*, illustrated by Bryan Collier.

As I introduced in *One Last Word*, the idea in Golden Shovel poetry is to take a short poem in its entirety, or a line from the poem, called a striking line, and to create a new poem using the words from the original. Say you decide to use a single line: you would arrange that line, word by word, in the right margin.

in

the

right

margin.

Then you would write a new poem, with each line ending in one of these words. In the example above, that would mean the first line of the new poem would end in the word *in*, the second line would end in the word *the*, and so on.

I wake and shake off the morning as Mom tiptoes **in.**
"Rise and shine," she whispers, always **the**
same old song. "Get up. **Right**
now!" I groan on cue, but she gives me no **margin.**

This is a very challenging way to create a poem, especially to come up with something that makes sense, and I love it for that very reason! In this form, the poet is bound by the words of the original poem, but the possibilities for creating something entirely new are exciting.

I continue to find this form a joy to create. I hope you'll give it a try, too!

—Nikki Grimes

PART I
HERITAGE

WHATEVER

by Nikki Grimes

Some days, I try to hide
my new woman body,
drape it in shirts
two sizes too big
to keep bug-eyed boys
from staring in my direction.
Other times, I get mad
if they don't look.
It's worse, though
when they act like
girls ain't nothin'.
I wish I didn't care
either way.
Today, Ms. Hicks, my teacher,
notices me hanging my head,
pulls me aside and tells me
I need to find
my "girl power."
I roll my eyes,
certain she's crazy
for imagining I got
any kind of power in me.

"I know you don't see it,"
she says.
What's she doing
reading my mind?
"Time you learn
a little history.
The women in our race
have always gone
from strength to strength.
Let me introduce you to
a few women who can teach you
what I mean."
She hands me three books
on the Harlem Renaissance.
"Whatever," I mumble
under my breath.
But I promise to read them.
Why not?
I've got
nothing better to do.

HERITAGE

by Mae V. Cowdery

It is a blessed heritage
To wear pain,
A bright smile on our lips.
Our dark fathers gave us
The gift of shedding sorrow
In a song.

BEFORE
by Nikki Grimes

Before we were women, we were **our**
Daddies' daughters, the **dark**
princesses who stole our **fathers'**
hearts. A single story says they **gave**
us little, except disappointment. But ask **us.**

Ask me and I'll chronicle **the**
currency of love Dad splurged on me, the **gift**
of "yes you can," and modeling dignity in the face **of**
vile attacks on his manhood without ever **shedding**
his humanity or surrendering to **sorrow.**

Like many dark fathers, he'd reclaim his soul **in**
the sweet strains of music, **a**
lesson we daughters learned: siphon sadness through a **song.**

I AM NOT PROUD

by Helene Johnson

I am not proud that I am bold
Or proud that I am black.
Color was given me as a gauge
And boldness came with that.

HAVING MY SAY

by Nikki Grimes

My mother named me Harmony hoping, **I**
suppose, for an acquiescent girl-child—which I **am**
not—some giggly shy soul satisfied with blending in, **not**
loud-mouthed, straight-talking me, **proud**
to speak my mind uninvited, whether **that**
proves less than wise in every circumstance. **I**
will grudgingly apologize if I **am**
occasionally wrong, but never apologize for being **bold.**

Mom sometimes shakes her head **or**
groans when I open my mouth, but Grandma is **proud**
of me for finding my voice so young, says **that**
since we live in a world where **I**
will routinely be unseen, unheard, unnoticed if I **am**
silent, I must speak because I am both girl and **Black.**

Who decided silence was a tax I must pay for my **color**
or gender? Since when **was**
intelligence the secret gift **given**
only to boys? If you ask **me,**
a girl living in this world has to be twice **as**
smart as any boy, especially if her skin's **a**
darker hue. Our words are worthwhile by any **gauge.**

So girls, speak up! I always do **and**
not just when I'm upset. It's silly to confuse **boldness**
with anger. For me, boldness is a requirement that **came**
as part of my Black-girl package, along **with**
my sass, and my bodacious hip-swing! Believe **that.**

I SIT AND SEW

by Alice Dunbar-Nelson

I sit and sew—a useless task it seems,
My hands grown tired, my head weighed down with dreams—
The panoply of war, the martial tread of men,
Grim-faced, stern-eyed, gazing beyond the ken
Of lesser souls, whose eyes have not seen Death
Nor learned to hold their lives but as a breath—
But—I must sit and sew.

I sit and sew—my heart aches with desire—
That pageant terrible, that fiercely pouring fire
On wasted fields, and writhing grotesque things
Once men. My soul in pity flings
Appealing cries, yearning only to go
There in that holocaust of hell, those fields of woe—
But—I must sit and sew.—

The little useless seam, the idle patch;
Why dream I here beneath my homely thatch,
When there they lie in sodden mud and rain,
Pitifully calling me, the quick ones and the slain?
You need me, Christ! It is no roseate dream
That beckons me—this pretty futile seam,
It stifles me—God, must I sit and sew?

ROOM FOR DREAMS

by Nikki Grimes

Answer this: Why must others choose my role before **I**
am even consulted? Am I to **sit**
silent at board meetings where I am CEO, **and**
let impudent men pretend I'm there only to **sew**
up the meeting's minutes? I'd sooner sew discord, **a**
pursuit more satisfying than the **useless**
or plain future men might assign me—a **task**
long on boredom, short on opportunity. **It**
might be wife, mother—honorable, but wrong for me, it **seems.**

Shouldn't I have a choice? Of course! **My**
tomorrows explode with the possibilities I see: my **hands**
strong and supple, sculpt. My scientific brain unfettered, **grown**
expansive enough to mend heart muscles, restore those **tired**
in mind and body. With no limitations, **my**
fantasies of a boundless future balloon inside my **head.**
If the stars cannot be measured or **weighed,**
why should a woman's potential be reduced **down**
to some miniature scale **with**
no room left for **dreams?**

JOY

by Clarissa Scott Delany

Joy shakes me like the wind that lifts a sail,
Like the roistering wind
That laughs through stalwart pines.
It floods me like the sun
On rain-drenched trees
That flash with silver and green.

I abandon myself to joy—
I laugh—I sing.
Too long have I walked a desolate way,
Too long stumbled down a maze
Bewildered.

LEAH'S REUNION

by Nikki Grimes

Yearly, I join the celebration of woman-**joy:**
the blessing of unchecked tears when calamity **shakes**
us, or when beauty surprises; the comfort of sisters cradling **me**
when Death slithers into the neighborhood, **like**
a rattler, striking yet another sweet son, **the**
promise of him broken. But there is also the cleansing **wind**
of deep belly laughter as we gather round **that**
love-worn kitchen table, licking morsels of each story that **lifts**
us. Without this maternal crew's guidance, **a**
brown girl like me would simply be adrift. No wind. No **sail.**

DUSK

by Angelina Weld Grimké

Twin stars through my purpling pane,
  The shriveling husk
Of a yellowing moon on the wane,—
  And the dusk.

VANISH

by Nikki Grimes

I could vanish, were it not for the **twin**
street lights outside my window, imitating **stars.**
Without their brightness, you'd peer **through**
half-open blinds and find barely an outline of **my**
blue-black body, skin **purpling**
toward midnight, my image invisible as a glass **pane.**

JEHOVAH'S GESTURE

by Gertrude Parthenia McBrown

All night long
Yielding bodies
Swayed
To the syncopated tunes
Of the jazzers.

Jazz-hounds everyone they were
As they poured their souls
Into the instruments of choice.

The fierce wind howled without,
Then, speaking in angry tones,
Shattered the window panes
And blew out the lights.
Zeus hurled his thunderbolts
And zigzagged the lightning through the dark.

The dancers' feet stood still;
The jazz-hounds were mute.

Angry winds,
Serpentine lightning,
Rolling thunder . . .
A crash!

A hurricane of souls . . .
The hand of God . . . in the dark.

JUDGMENT

by Nikki Grimes

Caged innocents, we study the heavens for **a**
lightning bolt of justice, a **hurricane**
of grace toward parents whose sole sin is love **of**
us and freedom. Our sin? Being labeled disposable **souls.**

PART II
EARTH MOTHER

EARTH, I THANK YOU

by Anne Spencer

Earth, I thank you
for the pleasure of your language
You've had a hard time
bringing it to me
from the ground
to grunt thru the noun
To all the way
feeling   seeing   smelling   touching
—awareness
I am here!

SWEET SISTER

by Nikki Grimes

Clay creatures, we forget our sisterhood with **earth**
as if we could survive without her nourishment. **I**
know better, but did I always? I **thank**
her now. Sink your teeth into a peach, and so will **you!**

Imagine a world without rosemary or rose, even **for**
a moment. Where would the flavor or **the**
fragrance be? How we'd miss the quiet **pleasure**
earth brings to nose and tongue, **of**
which we are not worthy. Earth, **your**
generosity deserves to be met with Love's **language.**

RONDEAU

by Jessie Redmon Fauset

When April's here and meadows wide
Once more with spring's sweet growths are pied,
   I close each book, drop each pursuit,
   And past the brook, no longer mute,
I joyous roam the countryside.
Look, here the violets shy abide
And there the mating robins hide—
   How keen my senses, how acute,
     When April's here.

And list! down where the shimmering tide
Hard by that farthest hill doth glide,
   Rise faint streams from shepherd's flute,
   Pan's pipes and Berecynthian lute.
Each sight, each sound fresh joys provide
     When April's here.

TARA TAKES ON MONTCLAIR

by Nikki Grimes

What's wrong with summer in the city? **I**
hate thinking of my friends, back on the block, **joyous**
in games of stickball without me, while I **roam**
some stupid street in Jersey with strangers I hardly know **the**
names of, just 'cause my folks want me to see "the **countryside.**"

Okay, there's endless green and an ocean of sky. So what? Then I **look**
at my cousins' house, swimming in grass—no concrete **here.**
Wait. They have a yard brushing up against a wall of trees? And **the**
grown-ups let us kids run wild? *Oops!*—we stomp Aunt Vy's **violets.**
"Let's head for the woods!" my cousins suggest. No longer **shy,**
I say yes. (Guess the countryside is something I *can* **abide.**)

1975

by Anne Spencer

Turn an earth clod
Peel a shaley rock
In fondness molest a curly worm
Whose *familiar* is everywhere
Kneel
And the curly worm   sentient *now*
Will *light* the word that tells the poet what a poem is

KNEEL

by Nikki Grimes

In search of verse, enter a garden and **kneel.**
Feel the sun-kissed clay between thumb **and**
forefinger. If you're surprised by **the**
wriggling life-form in the midst, a **curly**
brown creature, thank her for doing her **worm-**
work, turning your soil into gold—her **sentient**
sacrifice of time unmeasured, until **now.**

Meditate on the gifts the earth **will**
furnish, assuming nourishment, **light,**
and life's clear elixir— **the**
water which satisfies, soothes, tickles—what wet **word**
pours itself into the vessel **that**
you call thought? Be still till your imagination **tells**
you which picture it wants you to paint—this is **the**
lyrical word-journey of the **poet.**
Pace yourself. Watch the bee slowly gathering **what**
fragrant nectar he can find worthy of **a**
hive and its queen. Now, slowly, gather words for a **poem,**
a honey-glazed treat. Isn't that what a poem **is?**

OF EARTH

by Mae V. Cowdery

A mountain
Is earth's mouth . . .
She thrusts her lovely
Sun-painted lips
Through the clouds
For heaven's kiss.

A hill is earth's soul,
She raises her
Verdant joyous prayer
Unto the gods
On dawn-tinged thrones.

A river
Is earth's grief . . .
Tears from the hidden wells
Of her soul . . .

O Earth . . . . why do you weep?

SEEING

by Nikki Grimes

A place to row, to fish, scrub a dish, skip **a**
stone—worlds of possibilities reside in a **river.**

Can you see them? For a poor child, lack **is**
often what laps at the feet. It was for me, but **earth's**
scraps were more than evidence of poverty, or source of **grief**

to my mother's eyes. Over a pot, she'd slice wild onions, **tears**
streaming, add dandelion greens plucked **from**
patches of weeds outside our door, toss in **the**
herbs gathered weekly for secret recipes **hidden**
from the family, then feed us lip-smacking joy. **Wells**

of goodness from humble fare, the casual magic feat **of**
a mother known to redeem corn husks and scraps of cloth, creating **her**
own bits of beauty, routinely envisioned through the eyes of the **soul.**

AT THE SPRING DAWN

by Angelina Weld Grimké

I watched the dawn come,
　　Watched the spring dawn come,
And the red sun shouldered his way up
　　Through the grey, through the blue,
　　Through the lilac mists.
The quiet of it! The goodness of it!
　　And one bird awoke, sang, whirred
A blur of moving black against the sun,
　　Sang again—afar off.
And I stretched my arms to the redness of the sun,
Stretched to my finger tips,
　　And I laughed.
Ah! It is good to be alive, good to love,
　　At the dawn
　　At the spring dawn.

FAITHFUL

by Nikki Grimes

The punctured ozone layer bleeds radiation **and**
we offer complaint without apology for **the**
years of desecration Earth has suffered. **Red**
is no longer the color of jubilation, but warning: The **sun**
will now allow wildfires to run rampant. Nature **shouldered**
the brunt of man's mistreatment too long. Now it's **his**
turn to pay. Even so, it is the **way**
of creation to be faithful. Notice: Each dawn the sun comes **up.**

AUTUMN EVENING

by Ida Rowland

I love the wild, stormy beauty
Of a lake in autumn,
Like crumpled silver in the stinging winds—
Wild winds pregnant with slanting rain.

I love the silver dust of rising mist
Against the green and gray of dim shore lines,
The lonely call of some lost fowl,
And the croaking frogs in the falling dusk.

STRENGTH TRAINING
by Nikki Grimes

Cancer keeps trying to pin my mother to the mat **like**
a wrestler. But it's no match for her. However **crumpled**
up some weeks feel during chemo, she finds the **silver**
in each day—like the way our family crams **in**
more love for each other—Mom, Dad, my brother, and me. **The**
lesson learned in this fitful squall with its gray-tinged **stinging**
slant of rain? Cling to the good, despite the crushing **winds.**

PART III
TAKING NOTICE

UNSEEN

by Gertrude Parthenia McBrown

A dark old woman with weary feet
Struggled up the city street.

Weak and worn, but with heavenly look,
She clasped in her hand the Holy Book.

No one saw that the light in her eyes
Were angels' smiles from paradise.

No one helped her on her way,—
They were hurrying on to pray.

No one saw her drink the gall;
No one saw her gasp and fall.

She had climbed the mighty hill;
But no one knew her lips were still.

TAKING NOTICE
by Nikki Grimes

Her fingers gnarled, the moon mistakes **a**
woman's withered hand for part of a tree, **dark**
and invisible in a world where the **old**
weigh less than vapor, whether man or **woman.**
Upright or curled on the cracked sidewalk **with**
newspaper for a blanket, the homeless, **weary,**
go unseen, save for the stray dogs that lick their **feet.**

FLAG SALUTE

by Esther Popel

"I pledge allegiance to the flag"—
They dragged him naked
Through the muddy streets,
A feeble-minded black boy!
And the charge? Supposed assault
Upon an aged woman!
"Of the United States of America"—
One mile they dragged him
Like a sack of meal,
A rope around his neck,
A bloody ear
Left dangling by the patriotic hand
Of Nordic youth! (A boy of seventeen!)
"And to the Republic for which it stands"—
And then they hanged his body to a tree,
Below the window of the county judge
Whose pleadings for that battered human flesh

Were stifled by the brutish, raucous howls
Of men, and boys, and women with their babes,
Brought out to see the bloody spectacle
Of murder in the style of '33!
(Three thousand strong, they were!)
"One Nation, Indivisible"—
To make the tale complete
They built a fire—
What matters that the stuff they burned
Was flesh—and bone—and hair—
And reeking gasoline!
"With Liberty—and Justice"—
They cut the rope in bits
And passed them out,
For souvenirs, among the men and boys!
The teeth no doubt, on golden chains
Will hang
About the favored necks of sweethearts, wives,
And daughters, mothers, sisters, babies, too!
"For ALL!"

A MOTHER'S LAMENT

by Nikki Grimes

Ancestral blood waters cotton fields and the earth **I**
stand on, a history begun under lash, no **pledge**
of liberty until war forced it. My people's **allegiance**
to country was wrung from hearts of hope **to**
one day be treated equal to the sons of **the**
ones who shipped us naked to these shores, under freedom's **flag.**

THE BRONZE LEGACY (TO A BROWN BOY)

by Effie Lee Newsome

'Tis a noble gift to be brown, all brown,
   Like the strongest things that make up this earth,
Like the mountains grave and grand,
   Even like the trunks of trees—
Even oaks, to be like these!
   God builds His strength in bronze.

To be brown like thrush and lark!
   Like the subtle wren so dark!
Nay, the king of beasts wears brown;
   Eagles are of this same hue.
I thank God, then, I am brown.
   Brown has mighty things to do.

LIKE AN EAGLE

by Nikki Grimes

No one chooses his pigment, but note: **Eagles**
share the glistening shades of bronze my folk **are**
blessed with. This sun-drenched color is all the rage **of**
generations who've baked on beaches for a bit of **this**
glow. I know it's unseemly to boast. All the **same,**
I wouldn't trade my melanin skin for any other **hue.**

YOUR WORLD

by Georgia Douglas Johnson

Your world is as big as you make it.
I know, for I used to abide
In the narrowest nest in a corner,
My wings pressing close to my side.

But I sighted the distant horizon
Where the skyline encircled the sea
And I throbbed with a burning desire
To travel this immensity.

I battered the cordons around me
And cradled my wings on the breeze,
Then soared to the uttermost reaches
With rapture, with power, with ease!

MOTHER TO DAUGHTER

by Nikki Grimes

Eboni, the true unrealized promise of you is **your**
greatest asset. Yet, the gendered **world**
would keep it secret. The televised lie **is**
what this life sells, as sweetly **as**
honey on the tongue: your beautiful body, **big**
or small, is all. Your heart is measured **as**
nothing, your strength lightly weighed and—*Presto!*—**you**
find your horizons snipped as though you'd no wit to **make**
your own bold, broad, limitless choices. Have none of **it!**

Yes, it's tough to tune out the false voices. **I**
understand. But it is vital. Only you **know**
your potential. If unsure, listen **for**
the whispers of your heart. Look to your dreams! **I**
learned to find my full capacity reflected there, **used**
those dreams as guides **to**
chart my journey. At your age, though I was inclined to **abide**

the lies told about my limits, never daring to look **in.**
My idea of me shriveled until I was **the**
size of a new chick, small enough to wedge in the **narrowest**
spaces. I became a chirp-less bird, bound to the **nest**
until your grandmother told me I needn't be, that **in**
fact, I could fly, could soar if I had **a**
mind to. Then no one, or thing, could keep me in a **corner.**

Eboni, you are in every way **my**
child. You can fly, too. You simply have to find your **wings.**
Don't let the haters of the world continue **pressing**
them down. They'll clip your wings, if you let them get too **close.**
Don't. Decide which piece of sky you want **to**
own, and make your flight plans. **My**
money's on you, sweetie. I'll be right by your **side.**

FOUR WALLS

by Blanche Taylor Dickinson

Four great walls have hemmed me in.
Four strong, high walls:
Right and wrong,
Shall and shan't.

The mighty pillars tremble when
My conscience palls
And sings its song—
I can, I can't.

If for a moment Samson's strength
Were given me I'd shove
Them away from where I stand;
Free, I know I'd love
To ramble soul and all,
And never dread to strike a wall.

Again, I wonder would that be
Such a happy state for me . . .
The going, being, doing, sham—
And never knowing where I am.
I might not love freedom at all;
My tired wings might crave a wall—
Four walls to rise and pen me in
This conscious world with guarded men.

WHAT GIRLS CAN DO

by Nikki Grimes

Mr. Spencer thinks I don't notice the **four**
negative notions he constructs like **walls**
boxing us in: girls can't, shouldn't, won't, wouldn't. **To**
him, a girl's only purpose is helping a boy **rise**
to his potential—as if girls are devoid of skill **and**
promise. Ha! Men tried putting Shirley Chisholm in a **pen,**
Mae Jemison, and Misty Copeland, too—now **me?**
No! I'll decide what I'll be, what box—if any—I fit **in.**

PRELUDE

by Lucy Ariel Williams

I know how a volcano must feel
with molten lava
Smoldering in its breast.
Tonight thoughts, wild thoughts,
Are smoldering
In the very depths
Of my being.
I would hold them within me
If I could.
I would give them form
If I could.
I would make of them
Something beautiful
If I could.
But they will not be formed;
They will not be shaped.
I must pour them out thus,
Like molten lava.
Shape them into beautiful dreams
If you can.

I know how a volcano must feel.

SLOW BURN

by Nikki Grimes

It's a slow burn, the anger that simmers when **I**
am maligned for speaking the truth I **know,**
or daring to wear my woman-strength like a cape. **How**
it makes small men bristle and call me brazen! **A**
daily ration of such leaves me seething. The **volcano**
knows the smolder of that inner fire. I **must**
learn to harness the lava-like heat I **feel.**

ADVICE

by Gwendolyn Bennett

You were a sophist,
Pale and quite remote,
As you bade me
Write poems—
Brown poems
Of dark words
And prehistoric rhythms. . . .
Your pallor stifled my poesy
But I remembered a tapestry
That I would some day weave
Of dim purples and fine reds
And blues
Like night and death—
The keen precision of your words
Wove a silver thread
Through the dusk softness
Of my dream-stuff. . . .

BROWN POEMS
by Nikki Grimes

Literary magic rises from the alchemy of work, so **write!**
Use words to wring your heart out in syncopated **poems.**

Set your daydreams down in indelible ink, visions **brown**
as your skin, rich as the hue of you. Write chocolate **poems!**

Make each stanza strut. Imitate the hip-swing **of**
proud mamas sashaying across the page, **dark**
in their beauty, centuries of wisdom in their **words.**

JOURNEY'S END

by Nikki Grimes

I turn the final page
of the final book,
swallowing each word
of wisdom.
I breathe deep
and feel
something soft but strong
brushing once knobby
shoulder blades,
a quiet unfolding of feathery limbs
emerging from bone and skin.
I thank Miss Mae,
Miss Angelina, Miss Anne,
and all the others
for these new and mighty
glistening things
called wings.

They lift me
from the smallness
of other's
expectations,
reminding me
that I am more
than anyone
gives me credit for.

RESOURCES

POET BIOGRAPHIES

GWENDOLYN BENNETT, 1902–1981

Born in Giddings, Texas, Bennett attended Columbia University, graduated from Pratt Institute, and taught art at Howard University. Awarded a scholarship to attend the world-famous Paris art institute the Sorbonne, she left Howard, briefly, but resumed teaching upon her return. Based in Harlem, Bennett's passion for Black art and literature led her to become assistant editor of the magazine *Opportunity*, in which she wrote the literary column "The Ebony Flute." When editor Charles S. Johnson introduced "The Younger School of Negro Writers" at the famous Civic Club Dinner during the Harlem Renaissance, Bennett was among them, offering a special poem dedicated to the occasion. Bennett's poetry frequently appeared in literary magazines and journals, and was featured in Alain Locke's seminal anthology, *The New Negro*. Bennett never published a poetry collection of her own, but was influential in promoting, nurturing, and publishing Langston Hughes and other notable poets of the era. A member of the Harlem Artists Guild and director of the Harlem Community Arts Center from 1939 to 1944, Bennett remained active in the arts throughout her life.

MAE V. COWDERY, 1909–1953

Born in Philadelphia, Mae Virginia was the only child of her social worker mother and postal worker father. Her mother was an assistant director of the Bureau for Colored Children, later named the Bureau for Child Care. Cowdery attended the Philadelphia High School for Girls. In her senior year, she published three poems in *Black Opals*, a Philadelphia journal, and won first prize in a poetry contest run by *The Crisis*. She won another prize for a poem titled "Lamps." After graduation, she moved to New York City and studied at Pratt Institute. She settled in Greenwich Village and enjoyed cabarets both there and in Harlem. Widely published in *The Crisis* in the 1920s, she was one of the few women poets of the Harlem Renaissance to publish a volume of her work. The book was titled *We Lift Our Voices and Other Poems*. Encouraged by Langston Hughes and Alaine Locke, Cowdery nevertheless fell off the literary radar after 1936 and died in 1953.

Selected Works:
We Lift Our Voices and Other Poems (1936)

CLARISSA SCOTT DELANY, 1901–1927

She was born in Tuskegee, Alabama, to a father who worked for Booker T. Washington, who, doubtless, became an early influence. As a teenager, Delany was sent to New England to study at Bradford Academy, a Christian institute for women's education. She later entered Wellesley College where, playing field hockey, she became the first African American to earn a varsity letter at that school. She was a member of the debate team as well, and it was at the Boston Literary Guild that she discovered poetry, her true love. At the guild she was exposed to Claude McKay and other poets, writers, and artists of that time, who influenced the content and style of her writing. After graduating Wellesley, Delany traveled to Europe, visiting Germany and France for extended periods. Upon her return to the US, she moved to Washington, DC, where she nurtured her love of poetry by attending the literary salon of Georgia Douglas Johnson, as well as the Saturday Nighters Club, a literary society for the city's African American intellectuals. Delany published only four poems in her brief career. How remarkable that her work earned her a place among the poets of the Harlem Renaissance. Sadly, kidney disease stole her life at age twenty-six.

BLANCHE TAYLOR DICKINSON, 1896–?

Born in Kentucky, Dickinson was a Harlem Renaissance poet who burned brightly, but briefly. She attended Simmons University, then taught in Kentucky for several years. Meanwhile, she published poetry in *Opportunity*, *The Crisis*, *American Poet*, *Caroling Dusk*, and *Ebony and Topaz*. In 1927, her poem "A Sonnet and a Rondeau" was awarded the Buckner Prize. When she won the award, a photo of her appeared in the September 1927 issue of *Opportunity*. Though considered a true beauty herself, Dickinson's poems addressed the pain of Black women who feel invisible and ugly when compared to white standards of beauty. Her themes were powerful, and all too familiar. Unfortunately, after 1929 Dickinson seems to have disappeared from public record.

ALICE DUNBAR-NELSON, 1875–1935

Born Alice Moore in New Orleans, Louisiana, Dunbar-Nelson was of African American, Anglo, Native American, and Creole heritage. A poet, essayist, and diarist, she graduated from Straight University (now called Dillard University) and taught public school in New Orleans. In 1898, she met the poet Paul Laurence Dunbar. They married in New York and moved to Washington, DC. They separated four years later, and she eventually remarried twice. After her first marriage, she moved to Wilmington, Delaware, where she taught at Howard High School and the State College for Colored Students (now Delaware State College). She later taught at Howard University. Throughout this time, she kept busy writing and publishing essays, poetry, and newspaper articles. Very prolific, Dunbar-Nelson published her first book, *Violets and Other Tales*, in 1895 when she was just twenty years old. A second collection, *The Goodness of St. Rocque and Other Stories*, was published in 1899. Her writing touched on racism, oppression, family life, and work. In 1910, she coedited *A.M.E. Review*, and she published *Masterpieces of Negro Eloquence* in 1914. She edited *The Dunbar Speaker and Entertainer* in 1920 and published her poetry in *The Crisis*, *Ebony and Topaz*, *Opportunity*, and the Boston *Monthly Review*. An ardent activist, Dunbar-Nelson was an organizer for the women's suffrage movement and served as field representative for Woman's Committee of the Council of Defense (1918). She campaigned for the passage of the Dyer Anti-Lynching Bill, first introduced in 1918. In 2018, the US Senate unanimously passed a version of the bill titled the Justice for Victims of Lynching Act. The US House passed a revised version of the bill titled the Emmett Till Antilynching Act during the 2019–2020 session. The latest version awaits passage by the Senate and signature by the president. The poet also served as executive secretary of the American Friends Interracial Peace Committee from 1929 to 1931. Dunbar-Nelson died in Philadelphia in 1935.

Selected Works:

Violets and Other Tales (1895); *The Goodness of St. Rocque and Other Stories* (1899); *Masterpieces of Negro Eloquence* (1914)

JESSIE REDMON FAUSET, 1882–1961

Born in Camden County, New Jersey, and raised in Philadelphia, Fauset attended the predominately white Philadelphia High School for Girls, then won a scholarship to Cornell University. A member of the honor society and Phi Beta Kappa, Fauset went on to the University of Pennsylvania where she earned a master's in French. Master's degree notwithstanding, Fauset was unable to secure a teaching job in Philadelphia because of her color. Instead, she taught in Baltimore, Maryland, and Washington, DC. In 1912, while still teaching, Fauset began submitting reviews, essays, short stories, and poems to *The Crisis*. Founder W. E. B. Du Bois invited her to become the publication's literary editor, a job she accepted in 1919. In addition to nurturing the work of writers like Langston Hughes, Jean Toomer, and Claude McKay, Fauset continued her own writing, and coedited *The Brownies' Book*, a children's monthly magazine. Fauset also contributed translations of works written by French-speaking Black authors from Europe and Africa. In 1924, she wrote her first novel, *There Is Confusion*, a book featuring characters in a middle-class setting. The setting was considered unusual then—and still is—and Fauset found it difficult to find a publisher, though she eventually prevailed. She left *The Crisis* in 1926 and returned to teaching French at DeWitt Clinton High School in the Bronx. Moving forward, she concentrated on writing novels. *Plum Bun*, *The Chinaberry Tree*, and *Comedy: American Style* were the results. The success of her novels was mixed. Fauset is considered one of the midwives of the Harlem Renaissance. She died in Philadelphia at the age of seventy-nine.

Selected Works:
There Is Confusion (1924); *Plum Bun: A Novel Without a Moral* (1928); *The Chinaberry Tree* (1931); *Comedy: American Style* (1933)

ANGELINA WELD GRIMKÉ, 1880–1958

Born in Boston, Massachusetts, Grimké stepped into a legacy of social justice advocacy. Her father, Archibald Grimké, the second Black graduate of Harvard Law, was vice president of the NAACP, while her great-aunts, Angelina and Sarah Grimké, were prominent abolitionists who advocated for women's rights. Grimké had big shoes to fill. Her extensive education was key to achieving that, beginning with Fairmont Grammar School in Hyde Park in Boston, Massachusetts; Carlton Academy in Northfield, Minnesota; Cushing Academy in Ashburnham, Massachusetts; Girls' Latin School in Boston; and, finally, the Boston Normal School of Gymnastics (now Wellesley College). After graduating, she taught English in Washington, DC, until 1926. During that time, she began writing short stories, essays, and poetry published in *The Crisis, The New Negro*, and the anthologies *Caroling Dusk*, edited by Countee Cullen, and *Negro Poets and Their Poems*. Her play, *Rachel* (originally titled *Blessed Are the Barren*), with an all-Black cast, was created to support the NAACP's rally against the racist film *Birth of a Nation*. Her unapologetic and unflinching descriptions of lynchings and violence, in general, as well as her openly lesbian poetry, have kept much of her exhaustive body of work ignored, or unremarked upon. The world was not ready for Angelina Weld Grimké. She died in seclusion in 1958.

Selected Works:
Rachel: A Play in Three Acts (1920); *Selected Works by Angelina Weld Grimké* (1991)

GEORGIA DOUGLAS JOHNSON, 1880–1966

Born in Atlanta, Georgia, this poet eventually settled in Washington, DC, where she was swept up in the cultural high tide of the Harlem

Renaissance. A playwright, columnist, and poet, Johnson's verse was first published in *The Crisis*. *The Heart of a Woman*, her first book of poetry, appeared in 1918, followed by the popular, racially themed collection *Bronze* and two others. The musicality of Johnson's work reflects her years of study at Oberlin Conservatory and Cleveland College of Music and may explain why she was among the young Black writers formally introduced to the white literary establishment at a dinner in 1924. Johnson was one of the most highly anthologized female poets of the era, and she was among the first Black writers included in white mainstream publications like *Harper's* and *Century*. Johnson's DC home was a popular art salon where Renaissance writers frequently met to share ideas. In 1965, Atlanta University recognized Johnson's work with an honorary doctorate in literature.

Selected Works:
The Heart of a Woman (1918); *Bronze* (1922); *An Autumn Love Cycle* (1928); *Share My World* (1962)

HELENE JOHNSON, 1906–1995

Born in Boston and raised in Brookline, Massachusetts, Johnson grew up nurtured by a group of strong women who influenced her poetic voice. She was also no doubt influenced by noted novelist and short story writer Dorothy West, her cousin. While in Brookline, she joined the Saturday Evening Quill Club and won a short story contest in the *Boston Chronicle*. She attended Boston Girls' Latin School, then went on to Boston University, though she did not finish. In 1925, at nineteen years old, she published the first of many poems in *Opportunity*, which got her noticed. Johnson went on to publish in *The Crisis* and *Fire!!* In 1927, one of her most famous poems, "Bottled," was published in the May issue of *Vanity Fair*. That same year, Johnson and West moved to New York City, drawn by the creative energy of the Harlem Renaissance. Once in New York, she enrolled in classes at Columbia University, developing a friendship with writer Zora Neale Hurston along the way. Johnson's poetry explored race, gender, and the struggles of the economic and racial divide in Harlem, issues she was passionate about. Her work appeared in William Stanley Braithwaite's *Anthology of Magazine Verse* (1926), Countee Cullen's anthology *Caroling Dusk*, and James Weldon Johnson's *The Book of American Negro Poetry* (1931). Once she married William Warner Hubbell III and had a family, Johnson disappeared from the literary scene, but not before staking her claim as part of the historic moment that was the Harlem Renaissance. In fact, her work appeared in every major periodical and anthology of that era from 1925 to 1935. Her last published poems appeared in *Challenge: A Literary Quarterly* in 1935. Johnson died just shy of eighty-nine.

GERTRUDE PARTHENIA McBROWN, 1902–1989

Born in Charleston, South Carolina, McBrown studied at Emerson College of Drama in Boston and received her master's in education at Boston University. After graduation, she moved to Washington, DC, where she directed children's theater and published children's and adult poetry in *The Saturday Evening Quill*, a journal that also included the work of such notable writers as Dorothy West, Waring Cuney, and Helene Johnson. In 1935, she published *The Picture Poetry Book*, a collection for children. A founding member of Boston's Saturday Evening Quill Club, McBrown was also a playwright. She eventually moved to New York and studied in Europe and Africa. During her time in New York, she directed drama at the Carnegie Hall Studio and wrote a weekly column for a local paper in Queens. McBrown died in 1989.

Selected Works:
The Picture Poetry Book (1935)

EFFIE LEE NEWSOME, 1885–1979

Born in Philadelphia, Pennsylvania, Mary Effie Lee was the daughter of Mary Elizabeth Ashe Lee and Benjamin Franklin Lee, a bishop of the African Methodist Episcopal Church, and chief editor of *Christian Recorder*, the church's official news organ. During Newsome's childhood, the family moved to Ohio, where her father served as president of Wilberforce University. Intellectual pursuit was part of her DNA, and Newsome studied at Wilberforce, Oberlin, Pennsylvania Academy of the Fine Arts, and University of Pennsylvania. In 1920, she married Reverend Henry Nesby Newsome and moved with him to Birmingham, Alabama. After he died in 1937, she returned to Wilberforce and worked as children's librarian at Central State College, and the College of Education at Wilberforce. Surrounded by prominent African American intellectuals of her day, Newsome found herself drawn to children's literature. She established a children's column at *The Crisis*, under editor W. E. B. Du Bois, contributing both poems and drawings of her own to *The Crisis, Opportunity*, and other leading journals. In addition, she published *Gladiola Garden*, a book of her children's verse, in 1940. *The Poetry of the Negro*, edited by Langston Hughes and Arna Bontemps, included some of Newsome's adult poetry. However, her body of work focused primarily on poetry for children. Newsome died in 1979.

Selected Works:
Wonders: The Best Children's Poems of Effie Lee Newsome (1999); *Gladiola Garden: Poems of Outdoors and Indoors for Second Grade Readers* (1940)

ESTHER POPEL, 1896–1958

Born in Harrisburg, Pennsylvania, Popel graduated from Dickinson College in Carlisle, Pennsylvania, where she studied several languages and was a member of Phi Beta Kappa. She earned her degree and moved briefly to Baltimore, where she worked as a teacher. Later she moved to Washington, DC, and taught foreign languages to junior high school students. She married William A. Shaw, but wrote under her own name. They had one daughter together, though motherhood was not the only thing that occupied her time. In addition to caring for her family and teaching, Popel lectured on the state of race relations at various women's clubs and became a regular at the literary salons hosted by poet Georgia Douglas Johnson. During the Harlem Renaissance, Popel's poetry appeared regularly in the journals *Opportunity* and *The Crisis*. She wrote lyrical verse inspired by nature, as well as hard-hitting poetry about racism, lynchings, and other evils of her day. In 1934, she published a collection of poetry titled *A Forest Pool*. Popel died in 1958.

Selected Works:
A Forest Pool (1934)

IDA ROWLAND, 1904–?

Born in Texas, Rowland came in on the tail end of the Harlem Renaissance. A distinguished academic, she earned her bachelor's in 1936, and her master's in sociology in 1939, from the University of Nebraska-Omaha. She later attended Laval University in Quebec, where, in 1948, she became one of the few Black women of her generation to earn a PhD. Her single collection of poetry, *Lisping Leaves*, secured her place on the list of Renaissance poets. Her subject matter—migrating birds, coyotes, and rolling plains—reflects her heartland background. Other Harlem Renaissance notables emerging from this region include artist Aaron Douglas (Nebraska) and Langston Hughes (Kansas). For a time, Rowland was a professor at the University of Arkansas at Pine Bluff (formerly Arkansas AM&N). Upon retirement, she started a publishing company to produce books about African Americans, designed for young readers.

Selected Works:

Lisping Leaves (1939)

ANNE SPENCER, 1882–1975

Born in Henry County, Virginia, Annie Bethel Scales was the daughter of former slaves. She attended the Virginia Theological Seminary and College in Lynchburg, Virginia, where she excelled in reading and writing, but was weak in math and science. Fellow student Edward Spencer tutored her in those subjects while she helped him in his literary classes. After graduation, she taught in West Virginia, then returned to Lynchburg to marry Edward. They frequently hosted dignitaries like W. E. B. Du Bois, Gwendolyn Brooks, Langston Hughes, and Martin Luther King Jr., who were unwelcome in Jim Crow hotels and restaurants. Spencer served twenty years as librarian for Dunbar High School and helped establish Lynchburg's NAACP. After retirement, she spent long hours in the garden, which explains the curly worms, shale rock, spiders, and clods of earth that abound in her poetry. Spencer's first published poem appeared in the journal *The Crisis*, and her last in the 1931 spring edition of *The Lyric*. Additional work appeared in anthologies like *The Book of American Negro Poetry*

(1922) and *Caroling Dusk* (1927). Spencer was the first African American woman poet featured in the *Norton Anthology of Modern Poetry* (1973). She died of cancer at ninety-three.

Selected Works
Time's Unfading Garden: Anne Spencer's Life and Poetry (1977);
Anne Spencer: "Ah, how poets sing and die!," a collection of her poetry with commentary by Nina V. Salmon (2001)

LUCY ARIEL WILLIAMS, 1905–1973
(AKA ARIEL WILLIAMS HOLLOWAY)

Born in Mobile, Alabama, Williams nurtured twin loves: poetry and music, though music dominated. The daughter of physician-pharmacist Dr. H. Roger Williams and Fannie Brandon, a teacher and choir singer, Williams studied music at Fisk University in Tennessee, then earned a second degree at Oberlin Conservatory of Music in 1928, specializing in piano and voice. Williams had hoped for a career as a concert pianist, but few such opportunities were available to people of color at the time. Finding her path blocked in this area did not deter her from pursuing her other passion—poetry. She tried hard to get her work into print and finally succeeded. In 1926, her poem "Northboun'" was published in the journal *Opportunity*, where it won a prize. It went on to become her signature poem. Published in several anthologies, "Northboun'" remains one of the best poems of the period. The lyrical quality of her poetry came, no doubt, from her extensive background in music. Williams's poetry appeared in other journals of the Harlem Renaissance era, and later, in 1955, she published a volume of her own, entitled *Shape Them Into Dreams*. She succeeded at making a living as a high school music teacher, however, and became supervisor of music in the Mobile, Alabama, public school system. Williams died in 1973.

Selected Works:
Shape Them Into Dreams (1955)

ARTIST BIOGRAPHIES

VANESSA BRANTLEY-NEWTON attended both School of Visual Arts and Fashion Institute of Technology in New York, where she studied fashion and children's illustration. An artist swathed in retro chic, she loves all things vintage—especially books and clothes from the 1940s through the '60s—and it shines through in her designs, which run the gamut of fun and whimsical to stylish and sophisticated. She loves to add unique touches to her work, including mixed-media accents, collage, and hand lettering. As an illustrator, she includes children of all ethnic backgrounds in her stories and artwork. She wants all children to see their unique experiences reflected in the books they read, so they can feel the same sense of empowerment and recognition she experienced as a young reader. ("Taking Notice," p. 69.)

COZBI A. CABRERA is a multimedia artist. Trained as an art director, this Parsons School of Design grad left her dream job creating music packaging in New York to make handmade collectible cloth dolls (*muñecas*) in honor of her Honduran heritage. Her dolls were featured on the *Oprah Winfrey Show* and *Martha Stewart Living* and in the Land of Nod catalogue, among others, and they are collected by Oprah, Mariska Hargitay, Maria Shriver, and Julie Belafonte. Cozbi's illustrated titles include *Beauty, Her Basket,* which *Publishers Weekly* called "a quiet treasure" in a starred review; *Thanks a Million; Stitchin' and Pullin': A Gee's Bend Quilt; Most Loved in All the World,* for which she won a Christopher Award; and *Exquisite: The Poetry and Life of Gwendolyn Brooks.* ("Seeing," p. 55.)

NINA CREWS has been writing and illustrating for over twenty-five years. Her first book, *One Hot Summer Day,* drew inspiration from the children and neighborhoods of Brooklyn. Other books include: *The Neighborhood Mother Goose,* which was selected as an ALA Notable Book, a *Kirkus* and a *School Library Journal* Best Book, and one of New York Public Library's 100 Books for Reading and Sharing, and *Seeing into Tomorrow: Haiku by Richard Wright,* which was an NCTE Notable Poetry Book, a CCBC Choice, a *School Library Journal* Best Book, one of New York Public Library's 100 Best Books for Kids, and a Junior Library Guild Selection. Her most recent book is *A Girl Like Me* written by Angela Johnson. She is the daughter of children's book authors and illustrators Donald Crews and Ann Jonas. She lives in Brooklyn, New York, with her husband, her son, and one cat. ("Vanish," p. 33.)

PAT CUMMINGS was born in Chicago but grew up traveling with her military family all over the world. She has been writing and illustrating children's books since she graduated from Pratt Institute and is the author and/or illustrator of more than forty books. In addition to her art for the Coretta Scott King Book Award winner *My Mama Needs Me* by Mildred Pitts Walter, Pat's luminous work includes *Angel Baby; Clean Your Room, Harvey Moon!;* and the Boston Globe–Horn Book Award winner *Talking with Artists.* She teaches children's book illustration and writing at Parsons School of Design, the New School, and Pratt Institute. She lives in Brooklyn, New York. ("What Girls Can Do," p. 85.)

LAURA FREEMAN is a Coretta Scott King Illustrator Honoree. She drew the engaging artwork found in *Hidden Figures* by Margot Lee Shetterly, which was recognized with an NAACP Image Award for Outstanding Literary Work-Children, reached the *New York Times* bestseller list, and was listed in "Ten Books All Young Georgians Should Read." Her art has been honored by the Society of Illustrators in New York City and in the *Communications Arts Illustration Annual.* In addition to illustrating books, Laura's art can be found adding color and style to a wide range of products, including dishes, textiles, and greeting cards, and her editorial images are frequently seen in the *New York Times* and other periodicals. Originally from New York City, Laura now lives in Atlanta, Georgia, with her husband and their two children. ("Slow Burn," p. 89.)

JAN SPIVEY GILCHRIST is the award-winning illustrator-author of one hundred children's books. Dr. Gilchrist illustrated the highly acclaimed picture book *The Great Migration: Journey to the North* by Eloise Greenfield, a winner of the Coretta Scott King Honor Award, a Junior Library Guild Selection, an NAACP Image Award nominee, a CCBC Best Book, and a Georgia State Children's Book Award nominee. She won the Coretta Scott King Award for her illustrations in *Nathaniel Talking* and a Coretta Scott King Honor for her illustrations in *Night on Neighborhood Street*, both by Eloise Greenfield as well. ("Like an Eagle," p. 77.)

EBONY GLENN is an Atlanta-based illustrator who enjoys bringing stories to life with whimsical imagery. With a passion for the arts, great storytelling, and advocating for more diverse narratives in children's books, she aims to create illustrations that will foster a love of reading in young readers. She also loves to create joyful and heartwarming crafts to satisfy her endless need to always make new things. When Ebony is not giving in to her creative itch of art-making, you may find her lost in the pages of a good book, learning some new Hula-Hooping tricks, or going on an adventure with her pups. Ebony is also a member of SCBWI, and she is the proud recipient of the Wonders of Childhood Focus Fellowship given by AIR Serenbe, a nonprofit artist residency program of the Serenbe Institute. ("Mother to Daughter," p. 81.)

XIA GORDON is an Ignatz-nominated cartoonist and illustrator living in Brooklyn, New York. She grew up in Orlando, Florida, and graduated from the School of Visual Arts with a BFA in cartooning and illustration. She studied as a teaching-assistant intern at the Robert Blackburn Printmaking Workshop and was a visiting artist at the Center for Cartoon Studies. Her comic *Kindling* was published by 2dcloud and was named one of *The Comic Journal*'s Best Comics of the year. She also illustrated *A Song for Gwendolyn Brooks* written by Alice Faye Duncan. ("Leah's Reunion," p. 29.)

APRIL HARRISON of Greenville, South Carolina, is a self-taught and Coretta Scott King-John Steptoe Award–winning artist who is, by her own admission, "merely a vessel being utilized to instinctively create narrative, sentiment and observation." She is known for "With Closed Eyes," her testimony of walking by sight. Her original artwork is currently in private, public, and corporate collections worldwide. ("A Mother's Lament," p. 73.)

VASHTI HARRISON is the number one *New York Times* bestselling illustrator and author of *Little Leaders: Bold Women in Black History* as well as *Little Dreamers: Visionary Women Around the World* and *Little Legends: Exceptional Men in Black History*. She also illustrated *Hair Love*—the film version of which won an Oscar for best animated short film—and the Coretta Scott King Honor Book *Sulwe* by Lupita Nyong'o, among other children's books. Also a filmmaker and originally from Onley, Virginia, she earned her BA from the University of Virginia with a double major in media studies and studio art with concentrations in film and cinematography. She received her MFA in film and video from CalArts, where she snuck into the animation department to learn from Disney and DreamWorks legends. She is passionate about crafting beautiful stories in the film and kidlit worlds. ("Sweet Sister," p. 43.)

EKUA HOLMES is a native of Roxbury in Boston, Massachusetts, a neighborhood that continues to inspire her work. Her picture books include the Caldecott Honor book *Voice of Freedom* and the Coretta Scott King Illustrator Award winners *Out of Wonder* and *The Stuff of Stars*. She is a graduate of the Massachusetts College of Art and Design, and she is a recipient of many honors and fellowships, including a five-year appointment to the Boston Art Commission. Currently, Holmes serves as assistant director of MassArt's Center for Art and Community Partnerships, and she manages sparc! the ArtMobile, the institution's vehicle for community outreach. ("Before," p. 17.)

CATHY ANN JOHNSON received her BFA from Columbus College of

Arts and Design. She spent several years at Hallmark Cards, where she honed her skills crafting emotional content that speaks to children. Her ability to work in a range of styles merited her a position in Hallmark's Center of Excellence. Cathy Ann loves connecting words to pictures, and her whimsical and lyrical style focuses on layouts that echo a child's perspective. Her work has appeared in children's books and magazines, posters, home décor and gift items, and more. She currently works from a small Crayola box located in downtown Decatur, Georgia, as well as a satellite studio in Rome, Italy. In her spare time, Cathy Ann, her husband, and cute doggie enjoy roaming Rome, chasing castles in medieval towns, and enjoying history and the arts. ("Judgment," p. 37.)

KEISHA MORRIS is an illustrator living and working in Reno, Nevada. What she loves about her artistic process is creating characters whose personalities jump off the page while she fulfills the need to tell their stories. She earned her BFA in illustration at the Fashion Institute of Technology in New York and mentored with such renown illustrators as Sean Qualls, Selina Alko, and Dan Santat. She currently works as an in-house illustrator in the T-shirt design industry helping to bring clients' ideas to life. She is also a freelance writer and illustrator of picture books and a member of SCBWI. When she is not drawing, she loves spending time with her wife, daughter, and two crazy cats, Elphie and Ollie! ("Brown Poems," p. 93.)

DARIA PEOPLES-RILEY earned a BA in English from UC Santa Barbara, where she found herself shelving books in the library and reading the writings of many notable authors. After earning a master's in education and following ten years of teaching, Daria became a full-time author and illustrator. Her debut picture book was *This Is It*, and *I Got Next* was published a year later. Daria is also the illustrator of *Gloria Takes a Stand* by Jessica M. Rinker, a picture book biography about the life and work of Gloria Steinem. Daria lives in Las Vegas, Nevada, with her family. ("Tara Takes on Montclair," p. 47.)

ANDREA PIPPINS is an illustrator and author who has a passion for creating images that reflect what she wants to see in art, media, and design. Her work has been featured in *Essence* magazine, the *New York Times*, and *O, The Oprah Magazine.* She has worked with clients such as Bloomberg, Broadly, ESPN, the High Line, *Lenny Letter*, Lincoln Center, and the National Museum of African American History and Culture. Andrea is the author of *I Love My Hair, Becoming Me*, and *We Inspire Me*, and she is the illustrator of *Young, Gifted and Black* and *Step Into Your Power*. Andrea is based in Stockholm, Sweden. ("Room for Dreams," p. 25.)

ERIN ROBINSON studied fashion design at Parsons School of Design. She began her creative journey making costumes for television and movies in Los Angeles and then returned to New York to design for the Gap, the Children's Place, and other children's wear companies before reinventing herself and venturing into the illustration world. She loves working in a variety of tangible mediums but eventually segued into the digital world of drawing. Her work can be found in many well-known newspapers and magazines and in her first fully illustrated book, *Brave. Black. First.: 50+ African American Women Who Changed the World,* with Crown Books and the Smithsonian's National Museum of African American History and Culture. She divides her time between New York City and Washington, DC. ("Faithful," p. 59.)

SHADRA STRICKLAND studied design, writing, and illustration at Syracuse University, and she completed her MFA at the School of Visual Arts in New York City. She won the Ezra Jack Keats Award and the Coretta Scott King-John Steptoe Award for New Talent for her first picture book, *Bird,* written by Zetta Elliott. Shadra is passionate about promoting positivity through her work, and her ultimate goal as a picture book author and illustrator is to teach children how to live their dreams. She currently teaches illustration at Maryland Institute College of Art in Baltimore. ("Having My Say," p. 21.)

NICOLE TADGELL is an award-winning watercolor artist whose work spans more than thirty luminous picture books for children, including *A Day with Daddy* by Nikki Grimes. Known for creating realistic yet whimsical characters and scenes, Nicole's work has been honored by the Children's Africana Book Award, the Américas Award, the Arkansas Diamond Primary Book Award, and the Growing Good Kids Book Award. A resident of Massachusetts, Nicole speaks and leads workshops at elementary schools, libraries, bookstores, and art classes for people of all ages. She is also an advertising agency art director with more than two decades' experience in graphic design. ("Strength Training," p. 63.)

ELIZABETH ZUNON was born in Albany, New York, and grew up in the Ivory Coast, West Africa. As a little girl, she loved to draw, paint, make up dances, and play dress-up in a household that was never devoid of chocolate. As she grew up, she didn't really change! Elizabeth has returned to her Albany roots, where she explores a multicultural world through painting, silk-screening, collage, and pondering the endless possibilities of chocolate. *Grandpa Cacao* was her first authored-illustrated book, and a love letter to the grandfather she never knew. ("Kneel," p. 51.)

ACKNOWLEDGMENTS

Writing, in general, is a lonely business. Yet, a book's journey from first draft to publication is something of a team sport.

Many thanks to librarian Jenna Pontious, who enthusiastically helped me find and access rare research materials through the blessing of interlibrary loans.

Thanks to trusted reader, Amy Malskeit, and to my arts group, Montage, for feedback on early drafts of my poetry.

Thanks to educator Ed Spicer and editor Mary Kate Castellani for helping me flesh out a list of Black women artists to bring onboard. Thanks, also, to every artist who said yes to this project.

Thanks to agent Elizabeth Harding, my cheerleader-in-chief, for acquiring all the necessary permissions—no small feat in a book involving works by so many other poets.

Thanks to friends who recommended Harlem Renaissance poetry collections that were new to me. You know who you are.

It takes a village, ya'll.

SOURCES

Anne Spencer: "Ah, how poets sing and die!," Anne Spencer, with commentary by Nina V. Salmon, the Anne Spencer Memorial Foundation, 2001.

Black Nature: Four Centuries of African American Nature Poetry, edited by Camille T. Dungy, University of Georgia Press, 2009.

The Oxford Encyclopedia of Children's Literature, edited by Jack Zipes, Oxford University Press, 2006.

Selected Works of Angelina Weld Grimké, edited by Carolivia Herron, Oxford University Press, 1991.

Shadowed Dreams: Women's Poetry of the Harlem Renaissance, edited by Maureen Honey, Rutgers University Press, 2006.

We Lift Our Voices and Other Poems, Mae V. Cowdery, Alpress Philadelphia, 1936.

WEB SOURCES

https://aaregistry.org/story/effie-newsome-an-awsome-childrens-poet

www.blackpast.org/african-american-history/dunbar-nelson-alice-
ruth-moore-1875-1935

https://www.britannica.com/biography/Gwendolyn-Bennett

https://www.dclibrary.org/

https://www.encyclopedia.com/education/news-wires-white-papers-
and-books/bennett-gwendolyn-b

http://www.keyreporter.org/PbkNews/PbkNewsDetails/2201.html

www.literaryladiesguide.com/author-biography/jessie-redmon-fauset/

www.literaryladiesguide.com/author-biography/helene-johnson/

http://www.myblackhistory.net/Gwendolyn_Bennett.htm

http://029c28c.netsolhost.com/blkren/bios/delanycms.html

https://www.oxfordreference.com/search?source=%2F10.1093%2Facref
%2F9780195146561.001.0001%2Facref-9780195146561&q=Effie+
Lee+Newsome

www.poemhunter.com/angelina-weld-grimk/biography

www.poetryfoundation.org/poets/mae-v-cowdery

www.poetryfoundation.org/poets/alice-moore-dunbar-nelson

www.poetryfoundation.org/poets/anne-spencer

https://poets.org (Academy of American Poets)

https://poets.org/poet/effie-lee-newsome

https://prabook.com/web

POEM PERMISSIONS

Gwendolyn Bennett: "Advice" (page 91) courtesy of the Gwendolyn Bennett papers, Schomburg Center for Research in Black Culture, the New York Public Library.

Clarissa Scott Delany: "Joy" (page 27) courtesy of the National Urban League, *Opportunity: A Journal of Negro Life* (October 1926).

Angelina Weld Grimké: "Dusk" (page 31) and "At the Spring Dawn" (page 57) Angelina Weld Grimké Papers, courtesy of Moorland-Spingarn Research Center, Howard University.

Helene Johnson: "I Am Not Proud" (page 18) © by Helene Johnson. First published in *Saturday Evening Quill* (April 1929). Reprinted by permission of Abigail McGrath.

Anne Spencer: "Earth, I Thank You" (page 41) and "1975" (page 49) courtesy of the Anne Spencer House and Garden Museum, Inc., Archives.

The author wishes to thank the Crisis Publishing Co., Inc., the publisher of *The Crisis*, the magazine of the National Association for the Advancement of Colored People, for the use of Blanche Taylor Dickinson, "Four Walls" (page 82); Jessie Redmon Fauset, "Rondeau" (page 45); Effie Lee Newsome, "The Bronze Legacy" (page 75); Esther Popel, "Flag Salute" (page 70); and Lucy Ariel Williams, "Prelude" (page 87).

Alice Dunbar-Nelson, "I Sit and Sew" (page 23) and Georgia Douglas Johnson, "Your World" (page 78) are in the public domain.

For Mae V. Cowdery, "Heritage" (page 15) and "Of Earth" (page 53); Gertrude Parthenia McBrown, "Jehovah's Gesture" (page 34) and "Unseen" (page 67); and Ida Rowland, "Autumn Evening" (page 61), every effort has been made to contact all copyright holders. If notified, the publisher will be pleased to rectify any errors or omissions at the earliest opportunity.

INDEX